Simone
visits the
MUSEUM

By Dr. Kelsi Bracmort   •   Illustrated by Takeia Marie

Publisher's Cataloging-in-Publication data

Names: Bracmort, Kelsi, author. | Marie, Takeia, illustrator.
Title: Simone visits the museum / by Dr. Kelsi Bracmort; illustrated by Takeia Marie.
Description: Washington, D.C. : Mayhew Pursuits LLC, 2018.
Identifiers: ISBN 978-0-9995685-0-7 (Hardcover) | 978-0-9995685-1-4 (ebook) | LCCN 2017916755
Summary: Simone and her mother visit the Smithsonian National Museum of African American History and Culture (NMAAHC) where Simone misplaces something of value.
Subjects: LCSH Mothers and daughters--Fiction. | Family--Fiction. | National Museum of African American History and Culture (U.S.)--Fiction. | Washington (D.C.)--Fiction. | African Americans--Fiction. | Responsibility--Fiction. | BISAC JUVENILE FICTION / People & Places / United States / African American | JUVENILE FICTION / Lifestyles / City & Town Life | JUVENILE FICTION / Family / General | JUVENILE FICTION / Art and Architecture
Classification: LCC PZ7.B7155 Sim 2018 | DDC [E]--dc23

The text for this book is set in Poppins.
The illustrations for this book were rendered digitally.

In loving memory of my grandmother, Marcelline Bracmort
—K.B.

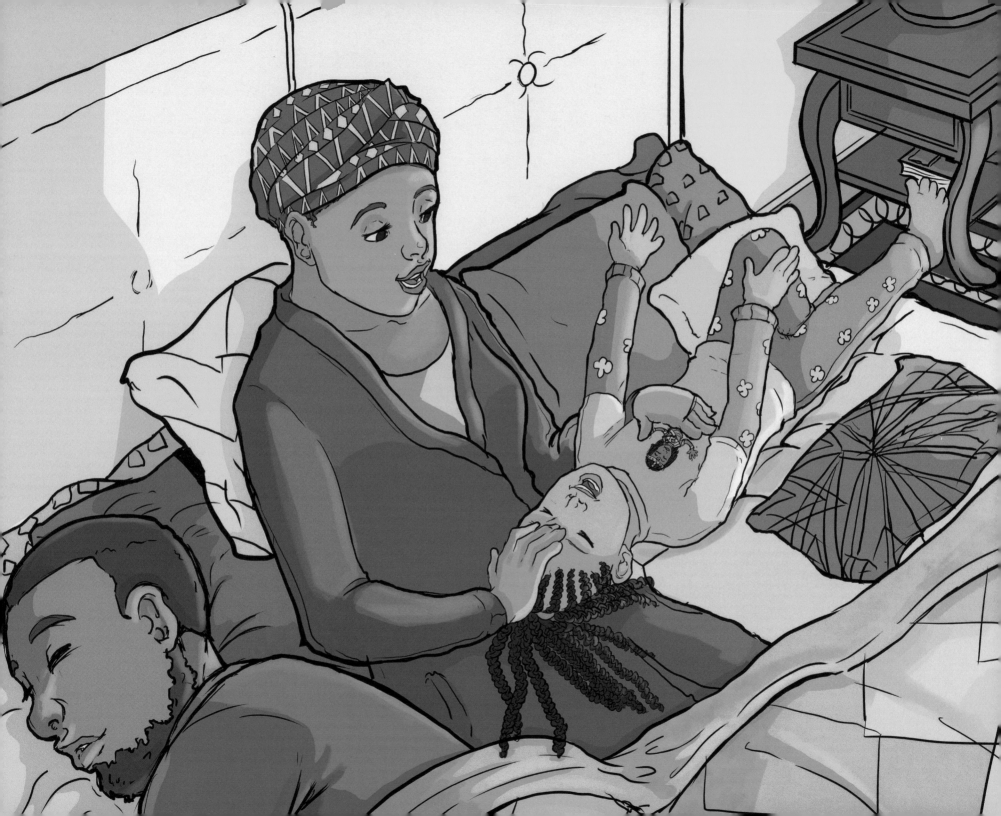

Early on a Saturday morning, Simone ran into her parents' bedroom, and hopped into bed to snuggle with her mother.

"Good morning my beautiful Simone!" her mother said smiling.

"Morning Mommy!" replied Simone.

Her mother kissed Simone on the forehead.

"It looks like today will be a beautiful day. Once you and your brother Scott finish breakfast, we will complete our chores, and then let's go explore our city."

"Okay!" Simone exclaimed.

SCOTT'S ROOM

At breakfast, Simone and her older brother Scott sat down to eat.

"Thank you, Mommy, for making my favorite oatmeal with cinnamon, raisins, and cranberries. Yum, it's so good!" Simone said.

Scott gulped down some orange juice and asked, "Can I add gummy bears to my oatmeal?"

"Eww! Yuck!" Simone said.

Their mother looked at both of them and said, "Scott, like I told you before, gummy bears are not for oatmeal, absolutely not, and Simone – you are welcome."

When they were done eating, their mother cleared the dishes from the table. "What chores do you want to do this morning?" she asked.

"I want to feed Sophie. I can separate my dirty clothes, so you can wash them . . . and I'll straighten up my bedroom." Simone replied cheerfully.

Scott sighed, "I'll wash the dishes and empty the trash can."

"Scott, straighten your room up as well. And, both of you, please work quietly so Daddy can sleep a little longer," said their mother.

Once she finished cleaning her bedroom, Simone joined Scott in the hallway. He had just come back from taking out the trash.

"I'm done! Can we go explore now?" Simone yelled.

Their mother walked toward them from the kitchen and replied, "Yes. We are going to take the bus to the Smithsonian National Museum of African American History and Culture, and then we can have a light lunch."

Scott shrugged, "I really want to work on my robot. Is it ok if I stay here with Daddy?"

"Sure," their mother said.

"Yes! Just me and Mommy!" shouted Simone. "Can I wear my red sneakers and my leggings and the new shades Daddy bought me?"

"Of course! Please, go get dressed," said her mother.

When they arrived at the National Mall, Simone and her mother walked along the gravel pathway towards the museum. They noticed lots of people having a good time. Some people jogged, some took pictures, and some played Frisbee.

They finally got to the museum and stood outside.

Simone squealed "Oh Mommy, this building is huuuuugggggge!"

"I agree. It is enormous. We'll probably need a museum map to help us navigate the collections and exhibitions," said her mother. "Now, do you remember how we behave in a museum?"

"Yes, yes, yes, yes. Stay near you at all times, lower my voice when speaking, greet the workers, and keep my hands to myself." Simone tried to whisper, but she was too excited and her words came out loudly.

"Okay, let's go enjoy," said her mother smiling.

Simone and her mother entered the museum and arrived at the welcome desk just in time to take part in a guided tour. Afterwards, they browsed the gift shop.

Simone and her mother didn't get to see every exhibit, but what they saw reflected the resilience and strength of African Americans.

As they started to leave the museum, Simone gasped just before they got to the door, "Oh no! Where are my shades? They're my favorite shades! Where did they go?"

"Don't worry," said her mother as she put her hand on Simone's shoulder. "I'm sure we can find them. Let's ask about a lost-and-found, and if we need to we can retrace some of our steps."

Simone and her mother walked back to the welcome desk when they were suddenly stopped by a smiling docent. He held in his hand her shiny glasses.

"Are these your shades?" he asked looking at Simone.

"Yes! Thank you so much. How did you know they were mine?" Simone asked.

"I saw them on top of your head when you walked into the museum. They're pretty shades and they sparkle. A visitor found them lying on a bench and gave them to me to take to the lost-and-found. Have a great day, and please come visit the museum again."

"We will!" Simone said happily as she put on her shades.

When they were outside, Simone skipped ahead. She didn't go far before she looked back at her mother, "That was fun Mommy! I learned so much. When you explained to me that families were separated during slavery, I started to miss Daddy and Scott. I want to know more. When can we come back?"

"I learned a lot, too. We will come back soon, and we can bring your Daddy and brother next time."

Simone exhaled deeply. "I guess that'd be okay." She loved Daddy and Scott, but she also really liked her time alone with Mommy.

"Are you hungry, Simone? I am starving and might faint if we don't eat something soon! Let's find some food."

Simone laughed and said, "Oh, Mommy, sometimes you are such a drama queen."

Her mother gave her a soft, but stern look, "Simone..."
Simone straightened up and said, "I'm just kidding."

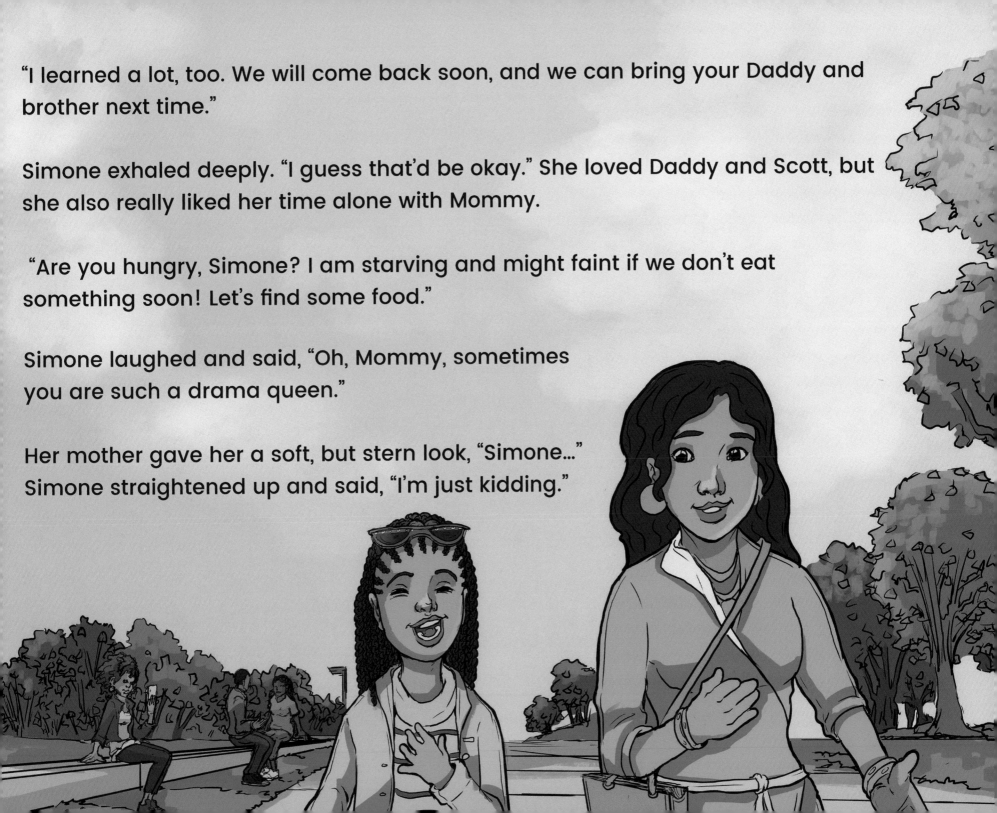

They found a café not far from the museum and sat outside.

Simone asked, "Mommy, what is the phrase you use when we eat outside?"

Her mother put down her sweet tea, "Al fresco dining."

Simone took a bite of her grilled cheese sandwich, "I like al fresco dining. There are so many cool people and unusual things going on as we eat."

Her mother poured dressing over her salad. "It's fine to look, but don't stare. After we finish our lunch, we can meet your Daddy and Scott at Anacostia Park, and share what we saw today."

Simone and her mother took the bus to the park. As they walked through the park, they saw families grilling vegetables and hamburgers. They also saw young men playing soccer and an all-female rowing club practicing on the Anacostia River.

"Look, there's Daddy and Scott! This day just keeps getting better," cried
Simone.

Her mother wrapped her arms around Simone's shoulders, kissed her on
top of her head, and said, "I'm glad we could spend this time together."

Simone looked up at her mother, and said, "Me too, Mommy."

ABOUT THE AUTHOR

Dr. Kelsi Bracmort loves living in Washington, D.C. and it is her hope that this book shows the pride, beauty, and diversity she sees in Washington, D.C. every day. It is her desire that this book will be one method to express to the children living in Washington, D.C. that they should take every opportunity to explore the entire city.

ABOUT THE ILLUSTRATOR

Takeia Marie is a freelance illustrator from New York who loves working with small businesses and individuals with big ideas. She hopes that this book will show the outstanding culture of Washington, D.C. and encourage children to explore the magic in their own backyard.

CPSIA information can be obtained at www.ICGtesting.com
Printed in the USA
BVIW12n1205080718
520590BV00002B/2